One for Me, One for You

A Book About Sharing

by Sarah Albee
illustrated by Karen Craig

Simon Spotlight/Nick Jr.
New York   London   Toronto   Sydney

Based on the TV series *Blue's Clues*® created by Traci Paige Johnson,
Todd Kessler, and Angela C. Santomero as seen on Nick Jr.®
On *Blue's Clues*, Joe is played by Donovan Patton. Photos by Joan Marcus.

 SIMON SPOTLIGHT
An imprint of Simon & Schuster Children's Publishing Division
1230 Avenue of the Americas, New York, New York 10020
© 2006 Viacom International Inc. All rights reserved. NICK JR., *Blue's Clues,* and all related titles,
logos, and characters are registered trademarks of Viacom International Inc.
All rights reserved, including the right of reproduction in whole or in part in any form.
SIMON SPOTLIGHT and colophon are registered trademarks of Simon & Schuster, Inc.
Manufactured in the United States of America
First Edition
10 9 8 7 6 5 4 3 2 1
ISBN-13: 978-1-4169-1300-9
ISBN-10: 1-4169-1300-9

Hi there! It's me, Joe. I'm glad you're here. Tomorrow is Sharing Day in Blue's classroom. Blue and I were just talking about what she should bring in to share with her class.

Oh! Great idea, Blue! We can play Blue's Clues to see what Blue wants to bring to her class for Sharing Day. Will you play too? Great! Keep your eyes out for Blue's paw prints. They'll be on the clues.

j51500

Look! Mr. Salt and Mrs. Pepper have a cookie for me and Blue! How thoughtful!

Hmmm. There are two of us and only one cookie. What do you think we should do?

Yeah! We could share the cookie! Let's break it into two pieces and we can each have a half! Great thinking!

Hey, do you see a clue?

It's . . . the color orange.
I wonder what orange thing
Blue wants to take to school
tomorrow for Sharing Day.

Let's go outside and see what
Shovel and Pail are up to.

Hi, Pail and Shovel! Hmm. Looks like both our friends want to play with the same toy.

Gee. What do you
think they should do?

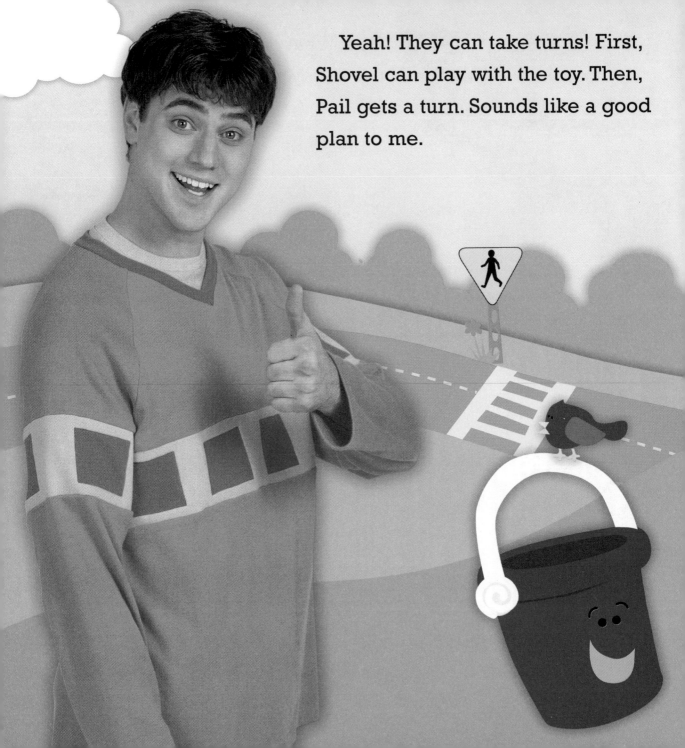

Yeah! They can take turns! First, Shovel can play with the toy. Then, Pail gets a turn. Sounds like a good plan to me.

You see another clue? Where?

We have our second clue. And it's a . . .

house. What do you think Blue wants to take to school tomorrow that's orange and has to do with a house?

Hi, bird friends! What's going on?

Hmmm. One bird has two seeds, one has one seed, and one has no seeds.

They want to divide their seeds, so they each have the same number. Gee. Will you help?

Oh! Great job, Blue! Blue sorted out the seeds and gave each bird one. Now they all have the same number of seeds!

Hey, did you see our last clue? It's a person! We have all three clues. You know what that means, right? It's time to go to . . . our Thinking Chair!

So our three clues are the color orange, a house, and a person.

Hmmm. What could Blue want to bring to school tomorrow that is a person, has the color orange, and has to do with a house?

Let's see. . . . Maybe the person wears the color orange and lives in a house. Like me! Hey, Blue, do you want to take me to school tomorrow? Yeah! She wants to take . . . me!

We just figured out Blue's Clues! I can't wait for tomorrow to come!

Now it's Sharing Day!

Blue's turn is next, and she's going to share me with he class! This is so exciting!

Hey, thanks for helping to figure out Blue's Clues. We had fun sharing with you. See you later!